Before You Were Mine

story by **Maribeth Boelts**   pictures by **David Walker**

G. P. Putnam's Sons

G. P. PUTNAM'S SONS

A division of Penguin Young Readers Group.

Published by The Penguin Group.

Penguin Group (USA) Inc., 375 Hudson Street, New York, NY 10014, U.S.A.

Penguin Group (Canada), 90 Eglinton Avenue East, Suite 700, Toronto, Ontario, Canada M4P 2Y3

(a division of Pearson Penguin Canada Inc.).

Penguin Books Ltd, 80 Strand, London WC2R 0RL, England.

Penguin Ireland, 25 St. Stephen's Green, Dublin 2, Ireland (a division of Penguin Books Ltd.).

Penguin Group (Australia), 250 Camberwell Road, Camberwell, Victoria 3124, Australia

(a division of Pearson Australia Group Pty Ltd).

Penguin Books India Pvt Ltd, 11 Community Centre, Panchsheel Park, New Delhi - 110 017, India.

Penguin Group (NZ), 67 Apollo Drive, Mairangi Bay, Auckland 1311, New Zealand

(a division of Pearson New Zealand Ltd.)

Penguin Books (South Africa) (Pty) Ltd, 24 Sturdee Avenue, Rosebank, Johannesburg 2196, South Africa.

Penguin Books Ltd, Registered Offices: 80 Strand, London WC2R 0RL, England.

Published simultaneously in Canada. Manufactured in China by South China Printing Co. Ltd.

Design by Katrina Damkoehler. Text set in Highlander.

Library of Congress Cataloging-in-Publication Data

Boelts, Maribeth, 1964– Before you were mine / Maribeth Boelts ; illustrated by David Walker. p. cm.

Summary: A young boy imagines what his rescued dog's life might have been like before he adopted him.

[1. Dogs—Fiction. 2. Pets—Fiction.] I. Walker, David, 1965– , ill. II. Title.

PZ7.B6338Bef 2008   [Fic]—dc22 2006020525   ISBN 978-0-399-24526-8

10 9 8

In memory of Lavern J. Boelts,
who gave many dogs a loving home. —M. B.

For Alex, the best dog ever. —D. W.

Before you were mine . . .

Did you live in a warm house with warm smells,
and a rug that was only yours?

Did you have a boy
who saved you the last bite of his cookie
and raced with you at the park?

Did you have another name—like Gus, or Sam, or Teddy, or Howie, or maybe Miles—before you were mine?

Was your boy proud when you learned a trick?

Did he talk about you at recess?

Or laugh when you licked his chin?

Before you were mine,
someone must have let you go. . . .

Maybe it was because they forgot
that puppies chew stuff

and pee on the carpet

and bark at birds.

Maybe they didn't know that
dogs like digging holes

and drinking from toilets

and hogging the bed
when it's stormy.

Before you were mine . . .
was someone mean to you?

Were you kept on a chain,
with a dusty bowl
and lonely sounds all around?

Did someone say, "Bad dog,"
even though it wasn't true?

Before you were mine, maybe a family loved you,
but they had to move and a guy at the new apartment
said no dogs allowed and he meant it.

Or maybe one day they left their gate open, and you ran away
and they never heard that if your dog runs away,
you look for him . . . until you find him.

Before you were mine,
the shelter told us that you had been
running for a long time . . .
eating whatever you could find,
which wasn't much.

Alone and scared, like a dog shouldn't be.

Did you sleep in dark alleys?
Did you dream of a boy?

Before you were mine, you were rescued.

They brought you to a place where
lots of other dogs waited.

They gave you a meal,

and a bath,

and a bed of your own.

But you weren't sure.

You huddled in the back of your cage . . .
shivering, with your tail tucked under.
The tag on your cage read, "Stray."

Before you were mine,
we had an old dog,
as worn-out and friendly as she could be . . .
and when we said our good-byes,
she wagged her tail one last time.

We sniffled and prayed and cried,
like there would never
be another dog who would love us just as much,
and who we would love, too,

but there was . . . you.

Before you were mine . . .
they couldn't have known what they had
in a dog like you . . .
or they would have never let you go.

So maybe it doesn't matter what happened
before you were mine . . .
because now,

you're *home*.

Adopting a dog from a shelter creates a ripple of hope. By welcoming a shelter dog into your home and into your heart, you have not just saved one life; you have also created additional room in the shelter for another dog in need of a forever family. While many people desire to adopt puppies, there are several benefits in adopting an adult dog. Their temperament has been established, you can see their grown size and general health, and they may have already passed through the challenging puppy behaviors like chewing.

Home for a shelter dog means a place where there is training, companionship, and most important . . . love—the kind of love that focuses not on what may have happened in a dog's life before, but on the hopeful potential of his future.

—Maribeth Boelts